Stuff on Paper

www.stuffonpaper.com

How Harvey and His Friends
Saved the Barn
D.L. Houseman

21849 Erdahl Court NE
Tenstrike, MN 56683
218-586-2212

ISBN: 978-0-578-01210-0

Printed in the United States of America
by
Arrow Printing
Bemidji, Minnesota 56601
LCCN: 2009902571

This story is dedicated to my grandchildren,
who by reading about Harvey and His Friends might
get to know their great and great great grandparents.

The Friends

How Harvey and His Friends
Saved the Barn

To: Jackson

WHEN YOU GROWUP... I WANT YOU TO LOVE READING and BE SURE
TO GO AND SEE A REAL BARN.

Written and Illustrated by D.L. Houseman   D. L. Houseman

LOOK and SEE IF YOU CAN FIND the 8 HIDDEN MICE IN
MY DRAWINGS

Out in the country, a very small group of very smart animals grew up together on an even smaller farm. Each of the animals were born and raised within the cozy stalls of the farm's wonderful old barn.

Barns, you see, are not just buildings on a farm in the country; they are like the churches you find in the city. These grand old structures offer animals comfort and trust. Very much like churches give comfort and trust to people.

Now, the animals who made up this very small group were: Ida the Chicken, Albert the Rooster, Lydia the Goose, Ben the Pig, Noma the Cow and finally Harvey the Horse. They all loved living in that grand old barn. This particular barn was built from a design that came from the country of Holland. The people from Holland were known as the Dutch. A Dutch designed barn has doors placed at both ends of the building, making it possible for each animal to easily enter and exit during the day and night.

In the middle of the barn, was a gray worn wooden ladder nailed against the wall. If you carefully climbed up this ladder, you'd find the barn's warm haymow. A haymow is where the owner of the barn would place his summer crop of hay. During the winter the owner would feed his animals by tossing down the food for the animals to eat. The haymow is where Ida the Chicken and Lydia the Goose chose to lay their eggs.

4

On the ground level of the barn, you would find Ben the Pig. This is where Ben had his marvelously messy old pen in the corner.

Albert the Rooster didn't have a corner, he perched on any post he liked

5

Noma the Cow loved her wooden stanchion with its worn smooth feel.

Last but not least, there was Harvey the Horse who had an abundance of straw to rest on each day.

6

Maynard the Farmer, who owned the farm, lived in his home a short tractor ride from the barn. He had taken care of the animals all their lives. This small family loved their grand old barn.

One day the wind blew and the bite of winter came through a broken window on the north side of the barn.

Noma the Cow shook and mooed her disapproval. "My! My! I don't remember it ever being this cold in here, especially at this time of the year." Noma the Cow always had something to say about the weather. The other animals simply pointed out to Noma the many missing pieces of glass all around the barn.

Ida the Chicken and Lydia the Goose clucked and squawked about what they had noticed as well. "My eggs almost rolled right through that huge gap in the haymow floor! They could have smashed into the gutter below," cackled Ida the Chicken.

9

Lydia the Goose hissed, "Well! I can see the night sky through the roof in the haymow where I nest each evening."

Sticking his pink snout
through the broken boards
in the corner of his pen,
Ben the Pig snorted, "I
think something needs to
be done about the poor
shape of our home."

Albert the Rooster certainly agreed as he crowed, "I can strut right through the holes made by all the missing boards in every single wall."

Totally dissatisfied, Harvey the Horse neighed into the conversation, "It appears our old home needs some help." What could the animals do? They could only talk among themselves. Maynard the Farmer knew each of his animals well, but he didn't speak Chicken, Cow, Goose, Pig or even Horse. They would have to find another way. But how?

That night, the animals went to bed thinking of all the ways they might show Maynard the Farmer that their grand old barn was in need of repairs.

In the morning, Ida the Chicken and Albert the Rooster were first to try. As Maynard the Farmer appeared below them in the barn, the two birds rolled two eggs through the hole in the haymow floor. Splat! Splat! The eggs hit the gutter just as Ida the Chicken had predicted. They narrowly missed Maynard the Farmer. He didn't even notice that eggs had fallen from a hole above his head!

With a big snort, Ben the Pig broke through the boards of his pen and trotted around the entire barn. He was squealing at the top of his lungs. Maynard the Farmer only pushed him back into his pen and shoved a scrap board into the broken space. Ben the Pig grunted in disgust.

It was now Lydia the Goose and Noma the Cow's turn to try. Noma the Cow struggled, and pulled her head from the stanchion, then with one toss she butted Lydia the Goose into the air with her horns. Flapping and squawking, Lydia the Goose flew straight through one of the missing windows.

Lydia's feathers flew in every direction and glass pieces showered all around. Once again, Maynard the Farmer didn't even notice the problem. He gathered up an old feed sack and placed it over the gaping hole. Noma and Lydia were not pleased at all!

Now, all the animals were very sad, because they thought they had failed. There was only one animal left to solve the problem. Harvey the Horse had thought all night long, and was still thinking outside in the cold barnyard. He loved this grand old barn. It had been his home for so long and just like the others, he had to try to save it.

How could he make Maynard the Farmer notice the broken windows, the missing boards and the gaping holes?

17

As Harvey the Horse slowly plodded in through the broken barn doors, there was still snow resting on his back. Just then an idea came to him! He did what came naturally.....he shook. Harvey the Horse did that funny horse shiver, where his whole skin shakes. Other animals can do it too, but Harvey the Horse did it the best.

18

Maynard the Farmer loved Harvey, and that is why he noticed right away how cold Harvey the Horse looked. He even noticed that Harvey's breath showed in the drafty, freezing air of the cold barn. As Maynard the Farmer gazed at the animals, they all appeared to be hunkered down in chilly poses.

Looking around, Maynard the Farmer was surprised! At last he noticed! There were gaps in the boards, broken pieces of glass and holes in the walls of his once grand old barn. It had taken his animals to show him how bad things had gotten. Right away, Maynard the Farmer went about making some patches in the walls and windows and some minor repairs to the doors. Now, this very small group of very smart animals would be warm for the rest of the winter.

However, the best was yet to come.

In the spring, the animals could see a special truck driving toward the farm. The huge truck carried Lyal the Carpenter and his son. They lived and worked in the nearby small town. Maynard the Farmer had called them to fix the barn.

The back of their truck was full of boards, nails, tools, windows, paint, tarpaper and new shingles. The minute they stepped out of the truck, the carpenters went quickly to work making repairs to the animal's barn.

The six animal friends sat quietly in the barnyard along with Maynard the Farmer and watched the two craftsmen work. Over the next few days, Lyal the Carpenter and his son restored the barn to the way that the very small group of very smart animals, and Maynard the Farmer remembered. And that is how Harvey and his Friends saved the barn.

The End.